Buster's day

Rod Campbell

CAMPBELL BOOKS

Buster finds lots to do
all day long.

'I'll help with the washing'
says Buster.

What can you see in the washing machine?

‘Now I’ll give kitty some milk’ says Buster.

What can you see in the fridge?

‘Now I’ll play hide and seek’
says Buster.

What can you see in the dresser?

'Now I'll play in the kitchen' says Buster.

What can you see in the tall cupboard?

‘Now I’ll have something to eat’ says Buster.

What can you see in the kitchen cupboard?

'Now I'll go into the garden' says Buster.

What can you see on the leaf?

‘Now I’ll look over the garden fence’ says Buster.

What can you see over the garden fence?

‘Now I’ll watch the birds’ says Buster.

What can you see in the nesting box?

‘Now I’ll play with the hosepipe’ says Buster.

What can you see in the flower bed?

‘Now I’ll have a nice bath’ says Buster.

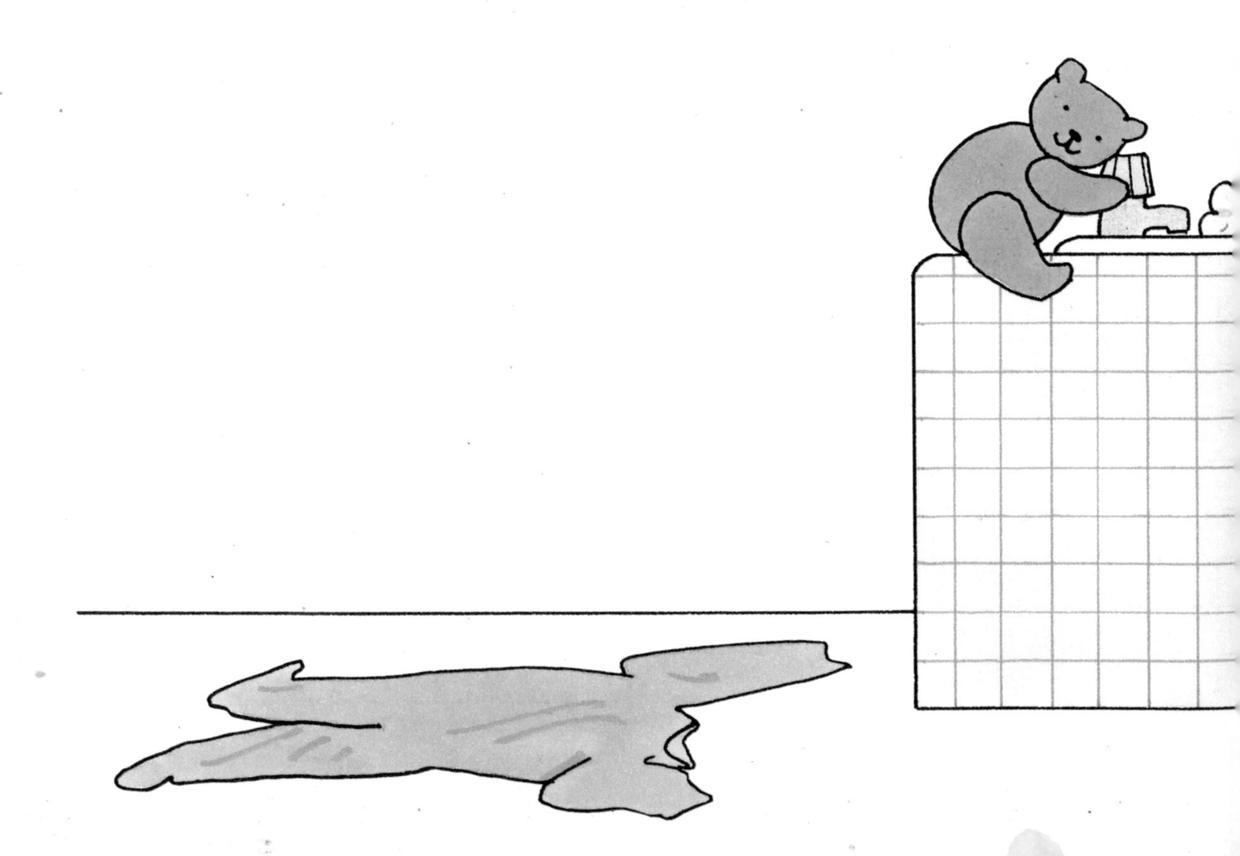

What can you see in the bathroom cupboard?

'And now I'll go to bed'
says Buster.

He gives a big yawn
and falls fast asleep!

What can you see through the window?

FOR THOMAS

First published 1988 by Campbell Blackie Books
Paperback edition published 1994 by Macmillan Children's Books
This edition published 1998 by Campbell Books
an imprint of Macmillan Children's Books
a division of Macmillan Publishers Limited
25 Eccleston Place, London, SW1W 9NF
and Basingstoke
Associated companies worldwide

ISBN 0 333 61206 X

3 5 7 9 8 6 4

A CIP catalogue record of this book is available
from the British Library

Printed in Singapore